MEGA MERLE
AND THE KITTEN CAPER

Written by Kate Scott
Illustrated by Becka Moor

OXFORD
UNIVERSITY PRESS

Words to look out for ...

extend *VERB*
To extend something is to stretch out.

master *VERB*
To master a subject or skill is to learn it completely or become able to do it well.

oppose *VERB*
To oppose someone or something is to be against them or disagree with them.

prior to *PHRASE*
Prior to means before.

realistic *ADJECTIVE*
If you think something is realistic, you think it can actually be achieved.

solid *NOUN*
firm or strongly made, rather than flimsy or fragile

typical *ADJECTIVE*
as you would expect from a particular person or thing; normal or usual

unnecessary *ADJECTIVE*
not needed

Meet the characters ...

ALEX

MERLE

MEGA MERLE

HAZEL

HURRICANE

COSMO

THE GERBILATOR

GERBILINOS

Chapter 1

"Merle!" Alex called excitedly, as she rushed into the bedroom.

Merle opened his eyes and yawned. He had been dreaming that he'd <u>mastered</u> the next level of his favourite game: Mega Missions.

"I have a surprise for you," said Alex.

Merle shook himself and jumped up. He LOVED surprises!

To <u>master</u> a subject or skill is to learn it completely or become able to do it well.

"Just wait!" Alex said, before running back out the door.

"I hope the surprise is a new bag of Nutty Nibbles!" thought Merle. "It's the most delicious hamster food EVER."

When Alex returned, she was holding a fluffy grey ball.

Merle scratched his head. It didn't look like a bag of Nutty Nibbles.

Alex came over to Merle's cage, holding the fluffy ball. Then she stroked it!

"Here we are, Cosmo," said Alex.

"Cosmo?" Merle thought.

"Meet Merle," Alex went on. "You're going to stay with Merle today. He'll help you feel at home."

Merle was confused. "What is going on?" he thought.

The fluffy ball stretched out a paw.
It was a kitten!

Merle was shocked. <u>Prior to</u> today,
he had been the only pet in Alex's
life. Now it looked like that was going
to change.

"I'm sure you two will be friends in
no time," Alex told them.

"OH NO WE WON'T!" thought Merle.
"I already have a friend ... Hazel!
I much prefer dogs to cats."

<u>Prior to</u> means before.

Alex sighed. "I wish our neighbours were going away for longer," she said, stroking the kitten. "I'd like to cat-sit you for more than two days, Cosmo."

"Two days!" thought Merle. "That sounds like forever!"

Suddenly Alex's mum called out. Alex placed the kitten on the bed, then picked up her school bag.

"Look after Cosmo, Merle!" Alex called as she left the room.

Merle heard the front door slam shut. He stared at Cosmo. "I can't look after a kitten!" Merle scoffed.

Cosmo opened his mouth and yawned. Then he curled back into a ball and closed his eyes. He began to purr loudly.

"Maybe this won't be so bad," thought Merle grumpily. "Maybe Cosmo will sleep all day. Maybe he'll sleep for two days. Then it'll be time for him to go home!"

Merle got a paperclip from the bottom of his cage. He unlocked the cage door. Stepping as quietly as he could, Merle made his way to the games console.

Merle tapped a button on the controller. The screen flashed to life and revealed the game: Mega Missions. Merle began to play. The level was hard, but he wanted to <u>master</u> it, like in his dream.

MEGA MISSION: COLLECT 10 SUPER SNACKS!

SUPER SNACKS: 9

He was only one Super Snack away from completing the level, when his fur prickled.

To <u>master</u> a subject or skill is to learn it completely or become able to do it well.

Merle spun round. Cosmo was looming over him.

"Can I play your game?" Cosmo asked politely.

Merle heard a crash. He turned back to the screen. His character had been squashed by a log. "That's typical," Merle said crossly. "I've been trying to get to the next level for weeks. I would have made it too, if you hadn't put me off."

Something that is typical is as you would expect from a particular person or thing.

"Pleeease can I play?" Cosmo asked.

"No way," Merle replied. "You don't know how."

"You could show me," Cosmo said, his whiskers twitching.

"It's too difficult for kittens," Merle told him.

"Fine," Cosmo said. "Then I'll find something else to do."

He jumped down and went out of Alex's room.

Chapter 2

Cosmo scampered into the living room. A piece of red fabric caught his eye. It was sticking out from behind a bookcase. He pawed the fabric, which turned out to be a cape and a mask. Cosmo's eyes widened. It was a superhero costume!

Cosmo tucked the cape into his collar. Then he put on the mask. It was a bit small, but Cosmo was too excited to care.

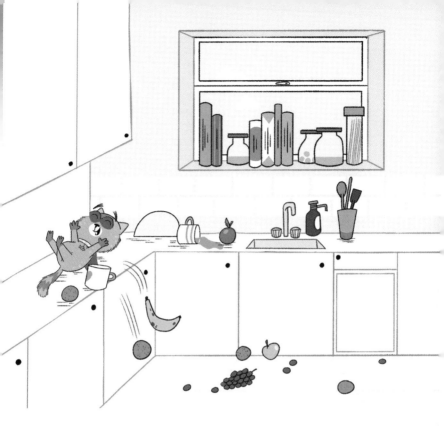

Cosmo pounced onto the kitchen worktop to practise some superhero moves. He dived and rolled, knocking things over as he went.

Then he spotted the window and the garden outside. He leapt across the cookbooks lined up on the windowsill to reach the handle. With one swift motion, Cosmo opened the window.

Meanwhile, Merle stared at the screen. He felt bad. Alex had told him to look after Cosmo. Instead, he had been selfish and mean.

"Cosmo!" Merle called, rushing out of the room. "I've changed my mind ... you can play the game. I'll teach you all my best moves!"

Merle ran into the kitchen. It was a mess.

"What happened?" Merle thought. Then he saw Cosmo's tail disappearing out of the window. "Oh no!"

Merle climbed up to the windowsill. He looked out to see Cosmo sliding down the drainpipe into the garden ... wearing his Mega Merle costume!

"Oh no!" Merle said again. "What if Cosmo gets lost? Or worse ... what if he runs into the Gerbilator?"

That would not be good. The Gerbilator was Mega Merle's number one enemy.

The kitchen mess would have to wait. Merle had to find Cosmo.

Chapter 3

Merle zoomed down the drainpipe into the garden. He saw a flash of grey disappearing into a hedge. Merle raced across the grass. When he got there, he couldn't see Cosmo. There was just a sign that read: *This is <u>NOT</u> the Gerbilator's hideout!*

This is <u>NOT</u> the Gerbilator's hideout!

Merle gulped. He knew the sign meant that the Gerbilator was nearby.

He needed to find Cosmo fast. However, if he was going anywhere near the Gerbilator, then he would need help ... and he knew just where to find it.

This is <u>NOT</u> the Gerbilator's hideout!

Merle ran back to the block of flats where he lived. He headed for Hazel's flat. Hazel was lying in her dog bed by the sofa. Merle knocked on the <u>solid</u> glass door.

Hazel looked up and wagged her tail excitedly when she realized who it was.

Merle signalled for her to come out and join him.

Something that is <u>solid</u> is firm or strongly made, rather than flimsy or fragile.

Outside, Hazel rushed up to Merle. "What's up?" she asked.

Merle told her everything that had happened that morning.

"Now I'm worried the Gerbilator has Cosmo. Will you help me find him?" Merle asked.

"Of course," replied Hazel.

"I don't have my costume," said Merle, "so you're going to have to ..."

"Get MEGA!" finished Hazel. She ran behind a bush and changed into Hurricane!

Hurricane

Merle led Hurricane to the hedge.
She began sniffing the ground. Hurricane
quickly picked up Cosmo's trail.

They stayed low as they crawled
through the hedge. They didn't want
to be spotted by any gerbils.

Suddenly, they heard voices close by.
Merle crept forward to get a better
view. He peered through the leaves.

Cosmo was on the other side of the hedge. Opposite him was the Gerbilator and three gerbilinos.

"Aww, don't you have anyone to play with?" the Gerbilator said. "Don't worry, you can play a game with us."

"What game?" Cosmo replied.

The Gerbilator smiled mischievously. "It's a little game I call Hide and Squeak," she said.

"How do you play?" asked Cosmo.

"That costume you're wearing belongs to my friend, Mega Merle," explained the Gerbilator. "Give the costume to me. We'll hide it so he can't find it."

"That doesn't sound very fun," replied Cosmo.

"Of course it is," the Gerbilator snapped. She turned to her gerbilinos. "And without his costume, Merle won't be so Mega!"

The gerbilinos giggled.

"Hide and Squeak! Hide and Squeak!" the gerbilinos sang.

"I don't know," Cosmo said, sounding unsure. "I think I should get back."

"Why would you want to do that?" asked the Gerbilator. "You said that Merle wasn't very nice to you."

"It doesn't matter," replied Cosmo. "I shouldn't have taken the costume in the first place."

The Gerbilator's smile disappeared, and her eyes narrowed. "There are lots of us," she said. "There is only one of you. Do you really think you can <u>oppose</u> us?"

The gerbilinos moved towards Cosmo. "Give us the costume!" one of them squeaked.

"No!" Cosmo said. "You can't have it." He edged backwards nervously.

To <u>oppose</u> someone or something is to be against them or disagree with them.

27

Merle crept forward and <u>extended</u> a paw. He tapped Cosmo's tail and whispered, "On the count of three, run!"

Cosmo's ears twitched. He gave a little nod.

Then Merle whispered, "One ... two ... three!"

Cosmo turned and ran under the hedge.

The gerbilinos pounced forwards and grabbed the cape. Cosmo felt a tug as it came out of his collar but he kept running.

To <u>extend</u> something is to stretch out.

The Gerbilator snatched the cape from the gerbilinos. "Get the mask from that kitten!" she shrieked.

The gerbilinos rushed after the heroes.

Merle, Hurricane and Cosmo darted out of the hedge. They ran across the garden and up a grassy slope. Merle spotted a large <u>solid</u>-looking log at the top.

"Follow me!" he said, darting towards the log.

Something that is <u>solid</u> is firm or strongly made, rather than flimsy or fragile.

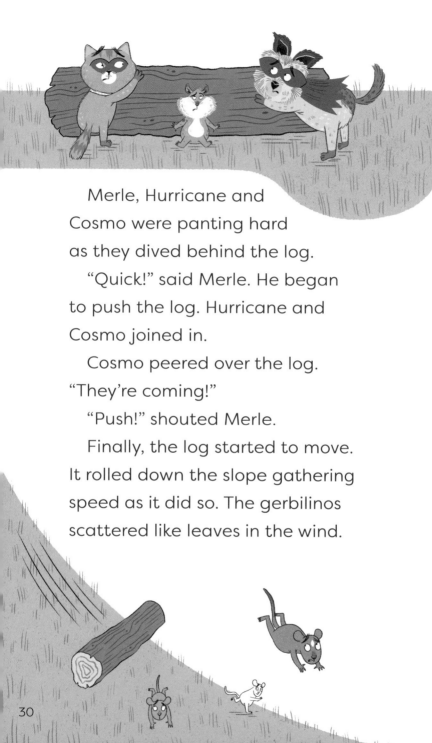

Merle, Hurricane and Cosmo were panting hard as they dived behind the log.

"Quick!" said Merle. He began to push the log. Hurricane and Cosmo joined in.

Cosmo peered over the log. "They're coming!"

"Push!" shouted Merle.

Finally, the log started to move. It rolled down the slope gathering speed as it did so. The gerbilinos scattered like leaves in the wind.

"That won't stop them for long," Merle said. "Let's hide!"

"Up there!" said Hurricane, pointing to a nearby bench. She leapt easily up onto the bench.

Merle <u>extended</u> his paws and jumped up. "I can't reach," he said.

"Hold on to my collar," suggested Cosmo. Merle grabbed on, and Cosmo leapt up, taking Merle with him.

They were safe ... for now.

To <u>extend</u> something is to stretch out.

Chapter 4

"I'm sorry I took your costume," Cosmo said.

"Your apology is <u>unnecessary</u>," replied Merle. "It should be me who's saying sorry ... I should have let you play my game."

"You were a bit mean," agreed Cosmo with a nod.

"I'll make it up to you," Merle promised. "When we get back, you can play the game as much as you like. You can even have first go."

If something is <u>unnecessary</u>, it is not needed.

"I have a better idea," said Cosmo.

"Oh?" said Merle.

"You can let me be part of your superhero team!" Cosmo said, striking a superhero pose.

"Erm ..." said Merle.

"Great idea!" cheered Hurricane. "You'll need a superhero name. How about Paws?"

"Hmm. How about Claws?" Cosmo suggested. "Or maybe ..."

"... The Claw!" Cosmo said. He lifted one of his front paws and <u>extended</u> his claws.

"Wow!" said Hazel. "Merle?"

"Fine, fine!" Merle said. "The Claw!"

Cosmo purred happily. He handed over Merle's mask. Merle put it on. Merle was starting to look like a superhero, just one thing was missing ...

"What about your cape?" Hurricane asked. "We must get it back from the Gerbilator!"

To <u>extend</u> something is to stretch out.

They peered through the gaps in the wooden bench. The Gerbilator and the gerbilinos were hunting round the garden. The Gerbilator was yelling. "Typical! Those cowards must be hiding. Find them, gerbilinos!"

Hurricane growled. "How dare she ... we're not cowards!"

"Shh," said Merle. "Don't let her upset you."

Something that is typical is as you would expect from a particular person or thing.

"What are we going to do?" whispered Cosmo.

Merle thought hard. The gerbilinos weren't big, but they were BIG TROUBLE. He looked around the garden and spotted a pile of rotting leaves in one of the flowerbeds.
He grinned. "I have a MEGA plan ..." said Merle.

Hurricane and Cosmo huddled close.

Chapter 5

"OK?" Merle asked his friends. They nodded confidently. "Off you go then, Hurricane."

Hurricane jumped off the bench and ran behind the pile of rotting leaves to hide.

"Your turn, Cosmo," said Merle. "Or should I say, The Claw?" Merle grinned and Cosmo grinned back.

The Gerbilator and her gerbilinos were standing by a giant oak tree.

"Good luck," whispered Merle.

"Thanks," Cosmo replied. "Here I go ..."

Cosmo leapt gracefully off the bench and walked over to the Gerbilator.

Merle listened closely.

"I've changed my mind," Cosmo told the Gerbilator. "I want to play Hide and Squeak."

"Is that right?" the Gerbilator said. "So where's the mask?"

"Oh, I've already hidden it in a really good place," Cosmo replied. "I'll show you. We can hide the cape there too."

The Gerbilator clutched the cape. "OK." She gave a nasty grin. "Merle will not be Mega for much longer!"

Cosmo led the gerbils towards the bench. When they were close, Merle leapt to the ground. "Time to get MEGA!" he yelled.

He landed right next to the gerbils, who scattered. All except the Gerbilator who stood there with her mouth open. Merle grabbed the cape and put it on.

Finally, he was Mega Merle again!

"Run!" Mega Merle cried to Cosmo. They dashed towards the flowerbed.

"After them!" screeched the Gerbilator.

Mega Merle and Cosmo ran past the pile of leaves where Hurricane was hiding ... then stopped.

The Gerbilator and her gerbilinos caught up. "We have you now," the Gerbilator sneered.

"I don't think so!" snapped Mega Merle. "Hurricane!"

Hurricane pushed the pile of rotting leaves over, which landed on the villains.

The Gerbilator poked her head out of the leaves, spluttering. "Gah!" she cried. "This is disgusting!"

"Looks like you're playing Hide and Squeak now, Gerbilator!" called Mega Merle.

Mega Merle, Hurricane and Cosmo giggled all the way home.

Chapter 6

The heroes climbed through a cat flap on the ground floor and ran upstairs.

Back at the flat, Merle took off his cape and mask. He found a new hiding place for them: under Alex's wardrobe.

"Can we play the game now?" Cosmo said.

"Sure!" said Merle.

"We should get snacks," said Merle. Hazel and Cosmo's eyes lit up. They all scampered to the kitchen but quickly came to a stop.

"Yikes! What happened in here?" asked Hazel, looking at the mess.

Cosmo didn't meet her eye.

"We need to tidy this up before Alex and her mum get home," said Merle.

"Is that <u>realistic</u>?" asked Hazel.

Merle didn't answer but looked at the clock on the wall. It read four o'clock. Alex would be back soon.

"Let's get to work!" he ordered.

Merle gathered all the food into a bowl. Hurricane swept the floor while Cosmo cleaned the worktops.

If you think something is <u>realistic</u>, you think it can actually be achieved.

Half an hour later, they had finished clearing up the mess.

"That was super teamwork!" said Merle. He checked the clock.

"I better go," said Hazel.

As Hazel headed home, Merle and Cosmo returned to Alex's room.

"We have time for a quick game of Mega Missions," said Merle. "What do you say?"

"I say, it's time to get MEGA!" said Cosmo, reaching for the controller.

"Thanks for saving me," Cosmo said.

"That's what superheroes are for," replied Merle.

"And friends?" said Cosmo.

Merle grinned. "Yes, and friends."

When Alex returned, she smiled. Merle was in his cage and Cosmo was on the bed.

"Look at you two!" she said. "You haven't moved all day!"

Merle and Cosmo grinned at each other.